Nick Ford Mysteries

Grave Robber

by
Jerry Stemach

Don Johnston Incorporated
Wauconda, Illinois

Edited by:

Gail Portnuff-Venable, MS

Speech and Language Pathologist, Scottish Rite Center for Childhood Language Disorders, San Francisco, California

Dorothy Tyack, MA

Learning Disabilities Specialist, Scottish Rite Center for Childhood Language Disorders, San Francisco, California

Ted S. Hasselbring, PhD

Professor of Special Education, Vanderbilt University, Nashville, Tennessee

Cover Illustration:

Karyl Shields, Jack Nichols

Interior Illustrations:

Phillip Dizick

Published by:

Don Johnston Incorporated.
1000 N. Rand Rd. Bldg. 115
PO Box 639
Wauconda, IL 60084

International Standard Book Number
ISBN 1-893376-00-1

Contents

This book is for Robert Gottsleben,
a friend and teacher.
Bob gave the gift of reading
to many, many people.

Many people have contributed to Grave Robber.
My wife, Beverly, and my children, Sarah and Kristie
my friends and colleagues
Ed and Lillian Hoch
Gail Portnuff-Venable and Dorothy Tyack
Karwarn Thorn and Erika Monroy
Don Johnston
the entire staff at Don Johnston Incorporated
Ted Hasselbring
Kevin Feldman
Michael Benedetti, Michael Sturgeon, Melia Dicker
Rachel Whitaker, Phillip Dizick
Greg Damron, Chris Clarke
John Palacek, Ellen Sweeney
Chuck Degagne
and the good people of Missouri.

Chapter 1
The Graveyard

"Someone dug up this grave!" shouted Ken.

"Shine your light over here," yelled Jeff. "This grave is dug up, too."

The boys looked at the grave. Next to the hole they saw a pile of fresh dirt. Someone had left an old baseball cap and cans of Mug Root Beer on top of the pile.

"It must be kids," said Ken. "Just kids messing around."

Jeff picked up the cap. He looked at the letters on it. "NY," he said. "New York Yankees." Jeff held the cap out to Ken. "This cap is for a big head," said Jeff. "It's too big for a kid."

"We're in Missouri," said Ken. "Most people here hate the Yankees. This should be a cap for the St. Louis Cardinals."

Jeff grabbed Ken by the arm. "Turn off the light," he said. "Someone is coming."

Ken looked out into the darkness. At first he only saw a few fireflies.

They looked like little lights. Then he saw a bigger light. Both boys froze. A big man was walking toward the graveyard. In one hand he held a lantern. In the other hand, he held a pick and shovel. A huge black dog walked next to him.

"I don't see a hat on that man," said Ken. "Let's get out of here."

"You're right about one thing," said Jeff. "He doesn't have a hat on. But I don't want to go yet. Help me up into this tree. Then you go back to the motel to tell my dad about this.

I'll meet you at the coffee shop."

"Are you crazy?" asked Ken. "What if that jerk has a gun? What if he comes at you with that pick?"

Jeff stopped him. "It's too late, Ken."

The man and the dog stood still. The dog was looking at the boys. It started to bark. The man held up his lantern. The light fell on his face. He had long, dark hair and a beard. One of his eyes looked all white.

Suddenly, he turned off the lantern.

The boys looked into the darkness.

The man and the dog were gone!

"Darn it!" Jeff muttered.

"We are out of here," said Ken.

Chapter 2
After Midnight

Jeff and Ken stood and waited outside Room 7 at the Gateway Arch Motel. The door opened. Out stepped Nick Ford, Jeff's dad. Nick had that look on his face. "I was on my way to find you two," he said. "It's after 2 o'clock in the morning."

"We met some girls," said Ken.

"And I met Batman," Nick said. They all laughed.

Nick trusted Ken and Jeff very much. They had been on many trips together.

Nick Ford was a teacher at City College of New York. Jeff and Ken were both students at City College. They wanted to be park rangers.

The Cancer Center in St. Louis had hired Nick to find some seeds of rare grass plants. The doctors at the Cancer Center thought that the seeds might cure cancer.

150 years ago the grass plants grew all over the Midwest, but now they were almost gone.

Farmers had destroyed them by planting corn, wheat, and oats, and by raising cows, sheep, and pigs. So now the grass plants were hard to find.

Nick and the boys thought that they could find the plants in old graveyards because no one had farmed in these old graveyards.

Nick turned back to the boys. "So where have you two been?" asked Nick.

"We have a problem," Jeff said.

Just then, the door to room 8 opened.

Two very pretty girls came out. One was Kris Ford, Jeff's sister. Kris smiled and tossed her long brown hair.
"In bed by midnight, remember?"
she said.

"We had a flat tire," said Ken. He winked at Kris.

"Yes," said Jeff. "Two girls in a sports car stopped to help us."

The other girl, Mandy Ming, laughed. She knew that Ken did not have a flat tire. Jeff, Kris, Ken, and Mandy were best friends. They had all met in college.

Mandy and Kris were roommates at the college dorm. Mandy wanted to be a doctor. Kris wanted to be a math teacher.

Mandy looked at the boys. “So what really happened?”

“We saw a grave robber,” Jeff said. “Some old man with a big dog is robbing graves.”

Jeff had that look in his eye. He was not kidding. For a moment, no one said anything.

Chapter 3

Bad Feelings in a Coffee Shop

The next morning Ken woke up early. He got dressed quickly and quietly. He grabbed a room key and stepped outside. The sun was still not up. Ken laced up his Nike running shoes and started jogging. Ken Rice was a tall, strong athlete. He ran five miles every day. He played football and baseball for City College of New York. He was a good student. He got good grades in his classes. Ken was African-American.

Ken ran down dirt roads past fields of corn. When he ran past the graveyard, he did not see anyone there.

Then he returned to the motel. Nick, Jeff, and the girls were just getting up.

"Let's go out to the graveyard right away," said Ken.

"Hold your horses," said Nick. "I need some coffee."

"And I need a jelly donut," said Jeff.

"And we need more sleep," said Mandy. She looked at Jeff. "You and Jeff kept us up all night. We kept thinking about big dogs."

"I told you," said Ken. "Mandy and Kris are slowing us down." Ken was teasing Mandy and Kris. They grinned.

Kris put her hand on Ken's arm. "You better wait for us, Ken," she said. "There's a dog with big teeth out there."

Ken laughed. "What will you do, Kris? Will you throw a jelly donut at it?"

Kris rode with Ken in his old Ford van. The others followed in Nick's Ford Explorer.

Ken's van was dented and rusty. The red paint was faded. Ken called his van "Ruby." Ruby had gone over 200,000 miles.

The coffee shop was crowded. Farmers sat at big round tables. Nick led the group to a small table in the back. The farmers looked up. Nick greeted them. "Good morning."

Not one farmer said "Good morning." Some of the farmers stared at Ken and Mandy. One farmer said something to Ken.

Everyone sat down. The farmers went back to their conversation.

"I have a bad feeling about this," Ken said.

"Don't worry," said Nick. "We're new here. These farmers don't trust strangers."

"It's more than trust," said Ken. "These men don't want us to be here."

Chapter 4

Show Me

Ken and Jeff took the others to the graveyard. They went back to look for the big hole. But it was gone! The dirt was flat and neat. The baseball cap and root beer cans were gone. Leaves were scattered around. The other grave looked the same way.

Mandy spoke. "Missouri is called the 'Show Me State.' So show me. I don't see anything."

"I'll show you," said Jeff. "The ground was dug up last night." He scraped away the leaves. Everyone could see the wet dirt.

Jeff told them about the baseball cap and root beer cans.

Nick looked at the gravestones. "Look at the name and date on this grave. Robert Beech. Born May 2, 1842. Died May 9, 1862."

Mandy looked at the other graves. "Something bad happened in 1862," she said. "These people all died in 1862."

Nick stood by a big oak tree. "Here is another grave. Tom Beech. He died in 1862. His grave was dug up, too."

"What's with these Beech boys?" asked Mandy.

Jeff smiled. "They died surfing," he said. "Surfing USA."

"Very funny," said Mandy. Everyone laughed.

"OK," said Nick. "It's time for a plan. And I have one."

Everyone gathered around Nick. He said, "Mandy and Kris, I want you to drive up to Hannibal. Go to the library there. Ask for a newspaper from June, 1862. And ask some questions."

"Hannibal, Missouri," said Kris. "Why do I know about Hannibal?"

"Mark Twain was born there," said Mandy. "He wrote Huck Finn and Tom Sawyer. Huck and Tom lived in Hannibal. It's right on the Mississippi River."

"Cool," said Kris. "We can see Mark Twain's house. We can..."

"No," said Jeff. "First find out about 1862 and the Beech boys."

"What about us?" asked Ken. "What do we do?"

"We are looking for grass seeds for the Cancer Center," said Nick. "Did you forget?"

Both boys looked sad. "Come on, Dad," said Jeff. "Someone is breaking the law. Robbing graves is a crime. We should stop it."

"We will stop it," said Nick. "We will find a good cop."

Chapter 5

The Grave Digger

It took Mandy and Kris one hour to drive to Hannibal. Hannibal, Missouri was a sleepy little town. One billboard said, SEE HUCK FINN'S CAVE! JUST $5.00!

"Huck Finn saw that cave for free," said Kris. "I hate rip-offs like that."

The girls drove past Mark Twain's house. Next to the house was a tall fence. It was painted white. "Tom Sawyer's fence," cried Kris. "Remember? He tricked his friends. He got them to paint it."

"Let's go to that coffee shop over there," said Mandy. "We can ask about a library."

"And we can eat," said Kris. "I need food."

The coffee shop was right beside the Mississippi River.

The girls went in and sat in a booth next to the window. A waitress came over to their table.

"Do you need a menu?" asked the waitress.

“I’d like Mississippi Mud Pie and coffee,” said Kris.

“Me too,” Mandy added. “Oh. And a library. We need a library.”

The waitress smiled. “There’s no library on the menu. The library is across the street from the Riverboat.” She pointed out the window. The girls could see the black smoke stacks of the Riverboat.

“Eat fast, girls,” said the waitress. “The library closes at 4:30.”

Mandy looked at the clock. It was 3:45.

The waitress quickly returned with the pie and the coffee.

"Mississippi Mud Pie is pure chocolate," said Kris.

"Chocolate with whipped cream and pie crust," added Mandy. "There's something from each basic food group."

Kris looked up and said, "I could eat..." Then she stopped.

"Are you OK?" Mandy asked.

Kris looked back at her pie. She shook her head. She reached into her backpack for a pencil. She wrote a note on her napkin. Then she said, "I could eat this pie for breakfast, lunch, and dinner." She gave the napkin to Mandy.

Mandy read it quickly. "Look at the man in the next booth. He has a big black dog and a baseball cap with New York Yankees on it!"

Chapter 6

Jack and Fang

Mandy dropped her fork. It fell off the table. Mandy turned and reached down for it. She heard a growl and looked up. She was staring into the drooling mouth of a big black dog.

The man grunted at the dog. “Fang! Get over here.” The dog just growled.

Mandy was shaking. She looked at the man. He was staring right at her with one eye. His other eye looked pale. It was looking off to the side. Mandy wanted to run. She tried to smile.

“Nice dog,” she said.

The man kept looking at Mandy. "Fang don't like no girls," he said. "Don't pet him."

The waitress brought more coffee. She looked at the man. "Don't you bother these girls, Jack." She looked at the dog. "That goes for you too, Fang."

The waitress smiled. She spoke softly to Kris and Mandy. "Jack is a no good drunk. The dog is a lazy flea bag."

"Do they live around here?" asked Mandy.

"Jack lives in a cave," the waitress said.

"There are lots of caves around here. He lives in a cave by the river."

"Where?" asked Kris. "Where is the cave?"

"Just south of here," said the waitress. "You can't miss it. Jack's cave is more like a junkyard. He needs a good flood. That would clean things up."

"Does he have a job?" asked Kris.

"I don't know," said the waitress.

"He pays cash in here. He's never left a tip. And the dog just stinks up the place."

The girls finished the pie in a hurry. It was nearly 4 o'clock. Kris stood up. "Come on, Mandy," said Kris. "The library closes in 30 minutes."

Mandy paid the bill. "We'll be back," she said. "That pie is to die for."

The waitress smiled. "I'm glad that you liked it. You kids come back again sometime," she said.

Outside Kris grabbed Mandy. Kris said, "Pie to die for? Don't say 'die,' Mandy. Not after meeting Jack and Fang."

Chapter 7

Death in 1862

The girls walked to the Hannibal Public Library. Inside the front door they saw a large photo of Mark Twain. In the photo, Twain was wearing a white coat. He was smoking a big cigar. Mandy read the card next to the photo. "Mark Twain was born across the street in 1835 as Samuel Langhorne Clemens. He died in 1910, famous around the world as Mark Twain. 1835-1910."

"I sure love that man," said Mandy.

"There's no time for love," said Kris. "We have work to do."

Inside they found the checkout desk piled high with books and papers. Behind the piles sat a plump lady reading a book. She did not see the girls.

"Excuse me," said Mandy in a low voice. There was no answer. The lady did not look up.

Kris tried. "Excuse me." Still no answer. Kris spotted a little brass bell. She rang it. The lady jumped in her seat.

"Oh!" she cried. "I'm reading about a murder. You scared me to death."

"I'm sorry," Mandy said. "We need a newspaper from June, 1862. Do you..."

The lady reached under her desk. Out came a little spool of film. She handed it to Mandy.

"It may look messy around here," said the lady. "But I know where everything is."

The girls knew what to do. They put the film on a reader. The reader showed the newspaper on a screen. They quickly found the papers for June, 1862.

The paper for June 20, 1862 told everything. On that day, 27 men were killed in the Civil War. Tom Beech and his 4 sons were killed. They were all buried in their uniforms. Now Kris and Mandy understood. The grave robber was looking for things from the Civil War. Old guns and medals and buttons were worth a lot of money. Kris turned off the reader.

"Come on," said Kris. "Let's get back to Nick and the boys."

But someone was watching them from a corner in the library.

Mandy could feel it. There! In the shadows! There sat Jack. He was staring at the girls with his one good eye. Fang showed his teeth and growled.

Chapter 8

Inside the Cave

The girls got into the Ford Explorer and locked the doors. Kris drove onto the main road. Mandy picked up the car phone. "I want to tell Jeff the news," she said.

She called the Gateway Arch Motel. The phone in room 7 rang and rang. "They're not at the motel," said Mandy. She punched in another number. "Maybe they're driving around in Ruby." The phone in Ruby rang and rang. Mandy hung up the phone. "There's no answer."

Just then Mandy held up her hand.

"Stop the car, Kris."

"What's the matter?" asked Kris. She slowed to a stop.

Mandy opened the door and got out. She reached under the seat. She grabbed their Nikon camera. "I have to get a look at Jack's cave. I'll meet you back at the motel." Mandy slammed the door.

Kris lowered the windows in the car. "Mandy!" she yelled. "Don't be stupid!" It was too late. Mandy was out of sight.

A big truck was coming up behind Kris. She stepped on the gas.

By now, Mandy was walking back toward Hannibal on the riverbank. Then she saw it. “Jack’s cave. The waitress was right,” said Mandy. Junk was everywhere. There were hubcaps from cars. Old windows were stacked by a tree. Bottles and cans were on the ground. Mandy picked up a can. “Mug Root Beer,” she read.

Mandy got out the camera. She looked through the lens. The camera made everything look much closer. She aimed it at the cliff. There in the cliff was an opening to a cave. Someone had painted some words on the rock. KEEP OUT! DOG WILL BITE!

Slowly she went closer to the cave. She picked up a small rock and threw it into the cave. There was no sound and no dog. Mandy stood up and went in.

Inside the cave, Mandy's eyes grew wide. She began taking pictures like mad. Old guns were leaning against the cave walls. She picked up a cigar box. It was full of old brass buttons and medals.

She took another picture and said, "Nick and the boys will be proud of me."

Mandy turned to leave. A growl came from the shadows. Mandy screamed. A white eye was staring at her. Fang was flying through the air. Mandy crashed onto the wet, cold ground with a thud.

Chapter 9

A Cop and a Clue

While Kris and Mandy were in Hannibal, Nick and Jeff and Ken were in the Pike County police station. Inside they met Buster Nelson. He was the only cop on the police force. Buster stuck out his hand. "I'm glad to meet you, boys," he said. Nick told Buster about the work for the Cancer Center. He told about looking for rare grass seeds in the graveyard.

"It sounds important," said Buster. "How can I help you boys?" He held an old, unlit cigar in his left hand. His belly hung over his gun belt.

"We think that someone is robbing the graves," said Jeff.

Buster frowned and said, "That can't be so. I drive by the graveyard two or three times a night."

Ken started to say, "Well, last night we saw..."

"You saw your own shadow, boy," said Buster. "Just shadows and graves." The cop patted his gun with his hand. He chewed on his cigar and spat into the trash can.

"The graveyard closes at 9 o'clock sharp," said Buster. "I don't let anyone out there past 9 o'clock. Not even you." Buster looked at Ken. "Spooks might get you," said the cop.

Nick nodded at the boys and said, "Well, thanks anyway, Buster. We made a mistake. We'll stick to the daytime from now on."

"You do that, boys," Buster said. "Leave the nighttime to me."

Ken put his hand out toward Buster. "Nice to meet you, sir." But Buster did not shake Ken's hand. Buster just stared. Then he spat again.

Nick, Jeff, and Ken went outside to their van. They all got in.

Jeff asked, "Did you see it?"

"What?" asked Ken. "Did I see what?"

"The empty cans of Mug Root Beer in the trash," said Jeff.

Nick put up his hand. "Now just hold on," he said. "I don't like Buster. But root beer cans in the trash don't mean very much."

"Then how about this?" asked Jeff.

Nick and Ken looked at Jeff.
Jeff was holding up a paper. It was a map of the graveyard. Some graves were marked with an X. Jeff pointed to all of the X's. "Five of these graves have been dug up."

"You stole that paper?" screamed Ken. "From a cop? Are you out of your mind?"

Chapter 10

The Reason for Digging

Nick and the boys had dinner. At dinner they talked about a plan to stop the robber. They agreed that Buster would not be any help.

After dinner they drove back to the motel. They wanted to talk with Kris and Mandy.

They found Kris by the pool. She looked sad. She ran to her dad and hugged him. "Mandy isn't here," she said. She started to cry.

Ken put his arms around Kris. "Where is she?" he asked.

Kris told about Mandy and the cave. She told about meeting Jack and Fang. She told about the dead soldiers from the Civil War in 1862. "Mandy took the camera. She wanted proof about Jack," said Kris.

"Mandy is very brave and smart," said Jeff. "She will be OK."

Everyone was quiet. Then Nick spoke. "I only have one rule for you on these trips. Be safe. Don't go off by yourself. That's not safe. What if..."

Ken stopped Nick. "What did you find out, Kris?"

"The Beech boys were not even on the same side in the Civil War," she said. "Some people in Missouri fought for the South. They wanted to keep slaves. Some people fought for the North. They wanted to free slaves. Mr. Beech and Jim Beech were Yankees. They fought for the North. Jon and Robert Beech were Confederates. They fought for the South."

"Wow," said Ken. "Maybe they killed each other."

Jeff told Kris about Buster, the map, and the root beer cans. "I think that Buster and Jack are in this together," he said. "Buster keeps people away at night. Buster and Jack sell the Civil War stuff for big bucks."

"So now what do we do?" asked Kris.

"We call the cops in St. Louis," said Nick. "First, I want Mandy back safe. Then I want to stop the grave robber."

"How?" asked Kris.

"We have a plan," said Ken. "It starts at dark."

Nick looked at Kris. He put his hand on her back. "You are part of the plan, Kris," said Nick. "I want everything to go just right. Mandy is counting on us. Mandy's life may depend on us."

"Let's do it," said Ken.

Chapter 11

Lights, Camera, Action

By 9 o'clock that night Mandy still had not come back. She had not called the motel.

"I don't like it," said Nick. "But we have no choice. We have to go to the graveyard. We have to catch Buster and Jack. They will lead us to Mandy."

Kris and Ken drove the Ford Explorer. Nick and Jeff drove Ruby. They stopped far away from the graveyard.

"Kris, you stay here by the Explorer," said Nick. "We'll take the cell phone.

When we will call you, you turn on the signal light. Do you understand?" asked Nick.

Kris nodded. "I'm really worried about Mandy," she said.

"Let's take first things first," said Nick. "We will get Mandy."

Ken ran on ahead. He was wearing dark pants and a dark shirt. No one could see him.

Nick and Jeff waited. Then they followed Ken. No one spoke. There was only a sliver of a moon.

The gravestones gave Jeff goosebumps.

Ken sat behind the big oak tree. Next to the tree was a grave from 1862. It was on Buster's map. Ken waited. He thought about Mandy. "If they hurt her..." he thought. Just then, he stopped. A dog was barking close by. There were voices.

It was Buster. "Shut that dog up, Jack," said Buster.

Ken heard a chain. Jack was pulling on Fang's chain. Ken did not move.

"Dig here," said Buster.

Ken waited. It seemed like a long time. Then he heard a thud. Ken peered around the tree. Jack was standing deep in a hole.

"I've got it," said Jack. He reached down and picked up two old rifles.

"Those will bring $2,000 each," said Buster. "Hand them up."

Jack climbed out of the hole. Buster held up the guns. Jack was laughing. He was holding up a skull.

On the skull was Jack's New York Yankees baseball cap.

"I've got me a Yankee here," said Jack.

Ken slowly lifted his camera. He aimed it. Flash! He took their picture.

Chapter 12

Out of the Sky

At that moment, Nick punched the last number on the cell phone. Kris heard the ring. She turned on the signal light.

Ken jumped out from behind the tree. He ran straight at Jack. He hit Jack hard in the belly. The man fell back into the hole. Ken fell in on top of him. Ken heard the crack of old bones.

Buster reached for his gun. But Jeff came up from behind. He tackled Buster. "Eat dirt!" he yelled. Jeff grabbed Buster's gun. He held it at Buster's head.

Jack yelled at Fang. "Get him!" he screamed.

Fang's mouth was wide open. His eyes looked wild. He leaped at Nick. Fang's chain flew through the air with him. Nick was ready. Nick aimed a can of pepper spray at Fang. The dog fell to the ground and moaned. Then Fang ran blindly away.

Suddenly a chopper was over the graveyard. It was the St. Louis police. They turned on a big light. The graveyard was lit up. A voice spoke.

"This is the police. You are surrounded."

Jack and Buster looked up into the light. The police in the chopper had guns aimed at them.

Ken had his hands around Jack's neck. "Mandy!" yelled Ken. "Where is Mandy?"

Jack looked at Ken. He looked at Buster. Buster's face was in the dirt. "In...my...cave...on...the...river..." said Jack.

Nick was on the phone again. Now he spoke to the chopper.

"Heads up, boys," yelled Nick. A sack fell from the chopper. It landed in the dirt nearby. "Handcuffs," said Nick.

The chopper turned away. It was going toward the Mississippi River and Jack's cave.

The police found Mandy in the cave. Jack had tied her up with ropes. She was not badly hurt, but she was cold and scared.

By 11 o'clock, the chopper was back. It landed next to the graveyard. Two cops helped Mandy from the chopper. Two other cops ran to Nick and Jeff and Ken. The cops took Buster and Jack away. Fang was put into a cage.

Mandy shook her head. "I'm so sorry, Nick."

Nick hugged her. "You're safe, Mandy. Welcome back."

Chapter 13

The Farmer in the Red Hat

The next morning Nick took everyone to the coffee shop. "I am treating you all to jelly donuts," he said. They stopped by the door.

Ken pointed at the newspaper rack. "Look!" he said. He read the headline, COP IN JAIL. Below the headline was a photo of Jeff, Ken, Kris, and Mandy. Below the photo it said, "College students save old graveyard."

"You are heroes," said Nick. "And I am proud of you."

Nick opened the door to the coffee shop. There sat the same farmers at the same tables. Nick led the way to the back of the coffee shop. One farmer stood up. He started clapping. Then another farmer stood up. He clapped too.

Soon everyone in the coffee shop was standing. They were all clapping. Ken walked past the farmer in the red hat. The farmer patted Ken on the back. "Nice job," he said. "Thank you."

Ken shook the farmer's hand. Both men smiled.

Mandy sat down. "Well," she said. "We are heroes. It feels good. There's no more work for us. We can sit all day by the pool at the motel."

Nick smiled and said, "Remember the seeds? Remember the rare grass plants? Remember the Cancer Center? We will help find a cure for cancer. Then you can sit by the pool."

Jeff, Kris, Ken, and Mandy smiled. They shook their heads.

"OK," said Nick. "You may have one day off. But that's all. Then we get the seeds. And then we get back home.

I got another call last night. I leave on Sunday for another trip. Who wants to go with me?"

Just then the farmer in the red hat came over. "My name is Ben. Ben Beech. My Great Grandad is buried in that graveyard. Thank you for stopping Buster and Jack."

"We were glad to help," said Nick.

"All of the farmers are having a picnic today," said Ben. "It's a picnic for you. We want to say thanks.
Can you come?"

Nick smiled. "Well, Mandy?" he asked. "Do you want a picnic or a pool?"

Ben looked at Mandy. "That's easy. You can have both," he said. "We have a pool!

The End